The Adventures of Bambino
Bambino's Christmas Dream

The Adventures of Bambino
Bambino's Christmas Dream

by Thomas Jude Cypher

Illustrated by Art Mawhinney

Xulon Elite

Xulon Press Elite
2301 Lucien Way #415
Maitland, FL 32751
407.339.4217
www.xulonpress.com

Unless otherwise indicated, Scripture quotations taken from the King James Version (KJV) – *public domain.*

Paperback ISBN-13: 978-1-66285-731-7
Hard Cover ISBN-13: 978-1-66285-732-4
Ebook ISBN-13: 978-1-66285-733-1

Dedication

This book is dedicated to Our Lord and Savior, Jesus Christ, who is the Son of God. May the miracle of Jesus' birth, as told through the eyes of Bambino, encourage every reader to draw closer to Him. Thank You, Lord, for inspiring this story.

Words to Learn:

Manger - An open, wooden box used to feed animals.

Divine - Pertaining to, or coming from, God.

Savior - A person who saves another from harm or danger.

Mankind - All people; everyone.

Sin - Anything that God considers bad or wrong.

Forgiveness - To pardon someone who did something wrong to you.

Estranged - To be separated; a broken friendship.

Born Again - Having a new and stronger relationship with God.

Circumstance - A person's condition or situation.

Compassion - Feeling sympathy and concern for another's suffering.

It was Bambino's first Christmas
And he didn't really know
Why there was so much excitement
And packages with bows.

The night was Christmas Eve.
The house had sparkling lights,
And Bambino had a sense
This night was not like other nights.

Joyful Christmas music
Played on the radio.
Just outside the window
Was the gently falling snow.

Momma was in the kitchen
Preparing all the food
With a smile on her face
In her usual happy mood.

Bambino saw the table
Was set with pretty dishes.
He heard his family and the guests
Exchanging cheerful wishes.

There were many happy people
And the house was filled with glee.
Bambino noticed presents
Beneath the Christmas Tree.

Bambino also noticed
Some little figurines
With a baby in a manger
And people on their knees.

When Momma rang the dinner bell,
Everyone went to their seats.
Bambino ran to the dining room,
"Oh boy! It's time for treats!"

When everyone was seated
Daddy opened up a book.
Bambino saw "The Bible"
When he took a closer look.

Bambino listened closely
And soon became aware
That the birth of Baby Jesus
Was something very rare.

Daddy closed The Bible
And they bowed their heads to pray.
Then Momma served the meal
For this special holiday

When Christmas dinner ended,
They laughed and got along.
Then they heard, out on the porch,
The sound of Christmas songs.

Momma opened up the door
To hear the people sing.
Bambino saw it was the neighbors
Christmas caroling.

The songs were very similar
To the story Daddy read,
And Momma gave them cookies
Made from gingerbread.

She gave them all hot chocolate
And they went their merry way.
Bambino realized
Christmas is a special day!

As the dinner guests were leaving
The family hugged their friends.
Bambino loved Christmas Eve
And did not want it to end.

But Daddy said, "It's time to sleep"
So they got ready for bed.
Then Momma and Daddy
Kissed each one upon the head.

The children were excited
Because Santa comes tonight!
After "one *more* hug and kiss?"
Momma turned off the light.

The children talked of Santa
And each one took a turn,
But Bambino laid in bed
And pondered all the things he learned.

As Bambino drifted off to sleep,
The pup began to dream.
The images reminded him
Of things that he had seen.

He noticed Baby Jesus
And the people on their knees,
Just like the little figurines
Beneath the Christmas Tree.

As Bambino looked around,
He saw a donkey and some sheep,
But they did not make a noise
Since Baby Jesus was asleep.

He went up to the donkey
And asked, "Who is this child?"
The donkey looked at Jesus
And the donkey gently smiled.

"I journeyed with His parents,
Their belongings in a sack.
From Nazareth to Bethlehem
I carried Mary on my back."

"I heard them say, 'He is The King,
The King who's Most Divine.
He is born into this world
To be The Savior of mankind.'"

Bambino asked, "A King?
Then why isn't He able
To be born in a palace
Instead of this stable?"

"The Savior of mankind?
I'm not sure I understand."
So Bambino went to Mary
And gently nudged her hand.

Mary smiled at Bambino,
Love and kindness in her eyes.
She said, "His name is Jesus,
The Son of God Most High."

"The Baby's name means 'Savior',
The perfect name for Him,
Since God wants us to know
That Jesus saves us from our sin."

"He was born in this stable
Because there's no room at the inn.
A very humble way
For The King's life to begin."

"But it's the ideal place for Jesus
Since He's not the type of king
Who will live inside a palace,
Wearing crowns and golden rings."

16

"He won't seek earthly riches
Or desire to be great.
He'll be the humble Shepherd
Who leads us through Heaven's Gate."

"Mercy, Love, Forgiveness
Are the reasons that He came.
Jesus wipes away our guilt.
Jesus wipes away our shame."

Bambino turned to Joseph,
Who rubbed Bambino's head.
Joseph looked at Jesus
And Joseph softly said,

"Our sins keep us apart from God.
Mankind has been estranged,
But on this Holy night
Everything's about to change."

"For God so loved the world
That tonight He sent His Son
To carry-out His plan
Of forgiving *every* one."

"His love will take away our sins.
Jesus will be our friend,
And He was born for us
So that we may be born again."

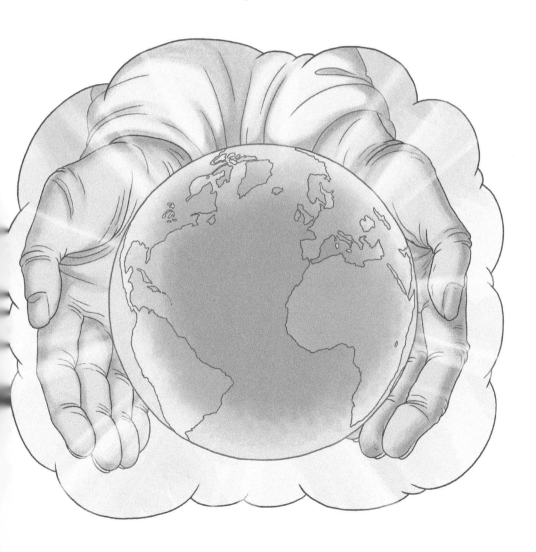

"God understands our weakness
And our sinful circumstance,
But His mercy and compassion
Give each one a second chance."

"God's forgiveness has no boundary!
His love will never cease!
God's Christmas gift is Jesus,
Who is The Prince of Peace!"

Bambino understood
What Mary and Joseph had to say
And they smiled at Bambino
As the scene faded away.

Bambino was awakened
By the family girls and boys
Who were running down the stairs
To open up their Christmas toys.

Momma served warm pastries
And they sipped on Christmas tea.
Even Bambino got a gift
That was underneath the tree!

The children opened Christmas gifts
In boxes big and small,
But Bambino knows that Jesus
Is the greatest gift of all!

The End

Shepherds were in the fields near Bethlehem. They were taking turns watching their flock during the night. An angel from the Lord suddenly appeared to them. The glory of the Lord filled the area with light, and they were terrified. The angel said to them, "Don't be afraid! I have good news for you, a message that will fill everyone with joy. Today your Savior, Christ the Lord, was born in David's city. This is how you will recognize him: You will find an infant wrapped in strips of cloth and lying in a manger." Suddenly, a large army of angels appeared with the angel. They were praising God by saying, "Glory to God in the highest heaven, and on earth peace to those who have his good will." (Luke 2:8-14)

Bambino's Lessons

Savior - Sin is unholy and dangerous. It separates us from God, Our Heavenly Father. Because God loves us so much, He sent His only Son, Jesus, to forgive us for our sins.

When you tell God that you are sorry for your sins, you are forgiven and reunited with God. Forgiveness repairs your broken friendship with God so you can go to Heaven. This is why Jesus is your personal Savior. (1 John 1:9; John 14:6; Acts 4:12)

Son of God - Jesus is God's only Son. Before coming to Earth and being born to Mary, Jesus lived in Heaven with The Father, The Holy Spirit, and the Angels. Since God the Father sent Jesus from Heaven, Jesus is the "begotten" Son of God, meaning that God is Jesus' true father, and Joseph is His "earthly father." (Matthew 3:16, 17; 1 John 4:15)

For God so Loved the World - Sin separates us from God, but God does not want us to be separated from Him. So how do we get back to God? Through Jesus' forgiveness.

People cannot do enough good deeds to take away our own sins, so Our Heavenly Father sent Jesus to take away our sins. God loved people ("the world") so much that He allowed Jesus to leave Heaven, be born of Mary, and eventually die on the cross so that the sins of everyone who ever lived would be forgiven. (John 3:16; John 15:13; Romans 5:8)

About the Author

Dr. Thomas Cypher, a native of Pittsburgh, Pennsylvania, currently lives in Salisbury, Maryland with his wife, 4 children, and Bambino. Dr. Cypher is a Podiatrist, a specialist of the Foot and Ankle. Having taught the Children's Liturgy at his church for many years, he is now a guest preacher at different churches. Dr. Cypher and his wife also read <u>The Adventures of Bambino</u> books to children at local schools and churches, where the children get to meet and interact with Bambino.

Dr. Cypher loves spending time with his family, reading The Bible, sports, and of course, playing with Bambino.

Lightning Source UK Ltd.
Milton Keynes UK
UKHW051457011122
411396UK00001BA/7